THE CHRONICLES OF
ARTHUR

SWORD OF
FIRE AND ICE

BY JOHN MATTHEWS
ILLUSTRATED BY MIKE COLLINS

ALADDIN

NEW YORK   LONDON   TORONTO   SYDNEY

To Mark Ryan, Mike Grell, and Rachel Pollack, who first showed me the power of graphic fiction—J. M.

To my wife, Karen, and our daughters, Bethan, Becky, and Rhainnon. Arthur had his not-of-this-world Nine, but I'm content with my fabulous four.—M. C.

ALADDIN
An imprint of Simon & Schuster Children's Publishing Division
1230 Avenue of the Americas, New York, NY 10020
First Aladdin hardcover edition September 2009
Text copyright © 2009 by John Matthews
Illustrations copyright © 2009 by Mike Collins
All rights reserved, including the right of reproduction in whole or
in part in any form.
ALADDIN is a trademark of Simon & Schuster, Inc., and related logo is a registered trademark of Simon & Schuster, Inc.
Also available in an Aladdin paperback edition.
For information about special discounts for bulk purchases, please contact Simon & Schuster Special Sales at 1-866-506-1949 or business@simonandschuster.com.
The Simon & Schuster Speakers Bureau can bring authors to your live event. For more information or to book an event contact the Simon & Schuster Speakers Bureau at 1-866-248-3049 or visit our website at www.simonspeakers.com.
Designed by Lisa Vega
The text of this book was set in WildAndCrazy.
The illustrations for this book were digitally rendered.
Manufactured in the United States of America
10 9 8 7 6 5 4 3 2 1
Library of Congress Control Number 2009926149
ISBN 978-1-4169-8683-6
ISBN 978-1-4169-5908-3 (pbk)

THE LONG STORY OF KING ARTHUR

This story is about King Arthur. It's not about the mythical King Arthur most people know; the one who lived in the Middle Ages, rescued beautiful ladies, fought the occasional giant, searched for the Holy Grail, and sat at a great round table with a hundred and fifty of his bravest knights before setting out on adventures.

The Arthur of our story is different. This Arthur lived nearly seven hundred years before the medieval king. In fact, he wasn't called a king at all. . . .

So who was he?

Our Arthur may not have been a king, but he *was* a hero—a warrior who led a ragtag army against a cruel invader.

The time: 537 AD.

The enemy: the Saxons—wild fighters from the Northlands who had set out to conquer the land of Britain.

You might be surprised to hear that this Arthur *really existed*! And although we don't know much about him, we do know that he was alive sometime at the beginning of the sixth century and that he was known as the most powerful leader of his time. Thanks to a few scraps of information written down by poets and monks who still remembered Arthur, we can say that he was a real person—one who's still written about to this day . . . more than fifteen hundred years after he lived!

To understand how all these events came about, we have to go back even farther in time, to when the Romans invaded Britain in the first century AD. At that time, the Romans established the farthest outpost of their empire in the cold lands of Britain. They stayed there for four hundred years, but in the end, when barbarians from the east threatened them, the Eternal City itself, the Romans left, leaving Britain unprotected and without a true leader.

After the Romans withdrew at around 410 AD, the tribes who had been their enemies turned on one another. Arthur was one of several native British leaders who emerged at this time. He was a mystery from the start. No one knows for certain where he came from. We do know, however, that Arthur managed to organize the feuding Celtic tribes into an army that was able to defend the land against a new threat: Saxons from Germany, Fresia, and Jutland.

With Arthur's command and leadership, the British forces drove the Saxons back to the coastline of the country and pinned them there for nearly forty years. During that time, the invaders became settlers, farming the land around the shoreline and marrying into British families. Eventually they founded a new race of people: the Anglo-Saxons, from whom most of the population of England is descended.

Although we know a bit about who Arthur was, we still don't know how or when he died. Stories suggest that he may have fought a final war against some of his own people. Arthur vanished from history around 545 AD, leaving a tale so powerful that it has gone on being told right up to the present time.

At first, the stories told about Arthur were simple accounts of his battles against the Saxons. But they gradually began to change. Elements of magic and fantastical new characters were added to the stories, and the myths and legends of Arthur were born.

Instead of a simple soldier's blade, Arthur now wielded Excalibur, a magical weapon linked with his destiny—the Sword of Fire and Ice in our story. When at one time he would have lived in a simple wooden building, Arthur now had the great castle of Camelot, where he and his knights met at a mighty round table large enough to seat a hundred and fifty.

Old tales of battle and bravery turned into powerful retellings, filled with strange and wonderful creatures and otherworldly characters, like the Lady of the Lake and Merlin, the wise and powerful magician who was often in the background helping Arthur obtain his wondrous sword and protecting him from the evil plots of his bitterest foe—his own half sister, Morgana le Fay.

The truth is there is not just one Arthur; there are several. There's the Arthur of medieval romance and legend; the noble leader of a band of knights who came together at the great round table in Camelot. There are earlier Arthurs: a second-century Roman cavalry officer named Lucius Artorius Castus, and the Arthur of the sixth century, who bore the Roman title "Dux" (Duke) rather than "king" but who led a company of warriors into battle against overwhelming odds.

Arthur has remained a timeless and fascinating hero. As many as two hundred new books, movies, plays, and poems about him are published every year! There have been operas, musicals, TV series, radio adaptations, plays, and video games that draw inspiration from the Arthurian tales.

Despite all the wonderful and magical stories of the medieval Arthur, the older tales have always fascinated us. What was that earlier Arthur like? What adventures did he have? And, especially, what happened to him before he became king, when he was just a boy growing up in a dangerous time?

When we were asked to tell the story of a young Arthur, we decided to go back to these first tales, some of which have survived in odd, out-of-the-way corners, and to see if we could fill in some of the gaps in the later tales.

So began *The Chronicles of Arthur*.

Merlin had to be there, of course, and if, as all the stories later told, he was Arthur's teacher, what kind of things might he have taught? What mysteries would he share with his pupil? We also wanted to show how the old magic (the kind that another writer, C. S. Lewis, called "the deep magic from before the dawn of time") was still around in Arthur's day.

The setting is the land of Albion, one of the ancient names for Great Britain, as seen from the heart of the mysterious Golden Wood, and from the otherworldly island of Avalon, ruled over by a group of otherworldly women known as the Nine. As well as these mysterious, dreamlike places, many other real ones may still be visited today.

In our story there is no specified time period, although you may hear echoes of the sixth and thirteenth centuries as we follow the young Arthur and his companions through the wild and tangled woods of the Arthurian world.

So, here is a first adventure for the boy who would, one day, be king. We hope you enjoy reading it as much as we enjoyed telling it.

Join us now at the beginning of Arthur's adventures. Turn the pages and prepare to be lost, for a time, in a magical world where all things are possible and only the unexpected is sure to be encountered!

LONG AGO, IN A TIME BEFORE HISTORY, THE ISLAND OF BRITAIN HAD ANOTHER NAME: ALBION, NAMED AFTER THE GIANT WHO ONCE RULED THIS LAND. IN THAT TIME, MANY STRANGE AND TERRIBLE BEINGS DWELLED ON THE ISLAND, THE LAST SURVIVORS OF ANCIENT RACES WHO ONCE HELD SWAY ACROSS THE WHOLE WORLD. HERE, IN A PLACE CALLED BY SOME THE GOLDEN WOOD AND BY OTHERS BROCELIANDE, A GREAT ENCHANTER AWOKE AMID THE TREES AND DREW HIS FIRST BREATH. IN TIME THE WORLD WOULD KNOW HIM AS MERLIN, THE ARCHITECT OF A DREAM THAT WOULD NEVER DIE, A DREAM OF A GREAT KING AND A GREAT KINGDOM, OF A ROUND TABLE WHERE ALL WOULD BE EQUAL AND WHERE THE MIGHTIEST WARRIORS OF THE TIME WOULD SIT. . . .

BUT THIS LAY STILL IN THE FUTURE. BEFORE THE DAYS OF THE GREAT KING WERE THE DAYS OF A BOY, COMING TO TERMS WITH LIFE, LEARNING THE SECRETS OF THE ANCIENT LAND OVER WHICH HE WOULD ONE DAY RULE, EXPLORING THE MAGICAL REALM OF AVALON, WHERE NINE ANCIENT AND OTHERWORLDLY WOMEN WIELDED THE POWER OF LIFE AND DEATH AND WHO GUARDED A GREAT AND TERRIBLE SECRET. . . .

HOW TO TELL OF THE KING? HIS COMING WAS FORETOLD—I READ IT IN THE STARS! NOW ALL MEN SPEAK OF HIM. HE IS THE GREATEST OF HEROES, THE MIGHTIEST OF LORDS. BUT FIRST HE WAS A BOY AND I, HIS TEACHER.

I FOUND HIM. I BROUGHT HIM TO THE NINE. WATCHED HIM GROW UNDER SUN AND MOON AND STARS.

NOW HE IS KING. THE GREATEST KING THESE LANDS HAVE EVER SEEN—PERHAPS EVER WILL SEE.

AND I . . . ? I AM MERLIN. HE IS— HE WAS—HE *WILL* BE—ARTHUR.

I CAME TO THE ANCIENT ISLAND OF AVALON, HIDDEN FROM THE SIGHT OF MEN FOR A THOUSAND YEARS. HERE DWELT THE SISTERHOOD OF THE NINE.

OLDER EVEN THAN I, THEY WATCH OVER THE LAND OF ALBION WITH PIERCING EYES.

NOTHING ESCAPES THEIR ATTENTION, LEAST OF ALL MY OWN COMING. . . .

WE WILL CARE FOR HIM. WE WILL SHOW HIM TRUE MAGIC.

WAIL!

I SHALL RETURN WHEN HE IS TEN YEARS OLD. UNTIL THEN HE IS YOURS. . . .

THE KING IS MY FATHER?

YES. ONE DAY YOU MAY BE KING.

WILL YOU TEACH ME MAGIC?

MAGIC IS NOT FOR YOU, ARTHUR. HAVE YOU NOT LEARNED THAT MUCH IN AVALON?

EVERY DAY THEREAFTER I MET THE YOUNG ARTHUR IN ONE OF THE MANY SECRET PLACES WITHIN THE GOLDEN WOOD. HERE I DID MY BEST TO PREPARE HIM FOR THE DAYS TO COME, WHEN HE WOULD BE KING AND RULE OVER ALBION.

ALTHOUGH I WOULD NOT TEACH HIM ANY DEEP MAGIC, I SHOWED HIM MANY WAYS TO BE AT ONE WITH THE WORLD AROUND HIM. HE PROVED A READY PUPIL.

AT LAST I WAS ABLE TO SHOW THE BOY WHAT HAPPENED IN THE WORLD BEYOND AVALON AND THE GOLDEN WOOD. HERE HIS FATHER, KING UTHER, . . .

. . . FOUGHT BRAVELY AGAINST THE BLOOD-THIRSTY SAXONS FROM THE FAR LANDS TO THE NORTH AND THE EQUALLY DANGEROUS PICTS FROM BEYOND THE OLD ROMAN WALL. . . . BUT THESE WERE NOTHING TO THE DANGERS THAT LURKED BEYOND HUMAN SIGHT. . . .

SOON I SHALL BE OLD ENOUGH TO FIGHT WITH MY FATHER, THE KING. . . .

YOU ARE FAR FROM READY, CHILD. THERE ARE OTHER MATTERS OF WHICH YOU MUST LEARN.

IT IS TIME YOU LEARNED THE ANCIENT HISTORY OF ALBION. WATCH AND LISTEN.

BERCILAK . . . ?

THAT . . . WAS . . . MY NAME. . . .

WHAT HAPPENED? WHY DID THEY . . . CHANGE YOU?

I DISOBEYED THE NINE. THIS IS MY PUNISHMENT.

BUT . . . WHY HERE?

WHERE BETTER FOR A GREEN KNIGHT TO HIDE! I AM A GUARDIAN.

I DON'T UNDERSTAND. WHAT IS THERE TO GUARD . . . ?

I MAY NOT SPEAK OF THAT, YOUNG ARTHUR. YOU WILL KNOW WHEN THE TIME COMES.

ARTHUR. I MUST GO ON A JOURNEY. I HAVE NEED OF YOUR HELP. . . .

MERLIN, WHAT DOES THE GREEN KNIGHT GUARD?

IT IS NOT YET TIME FOR YOU TO KNOW THAT. FIRST WE MUST FIND A HILL, AND A TOWER THAT WILL NOT STAND. . . .

23

'ERE YOU ARE, MY LORD. ONE BOY WITHOUT A FATHER.

THE OTHER ONE CALLED 'IM THAT.

MY NAME IS MERLIN. I HEAR YOU HAVE A PROBLEM.

YOU SEEM TO KNOW A LOT FOR ONE SO YOUNG.

THAT'S BECAUSE I'M CLEVER, MY LORD.

KILL HIM NOW!

IF YOU DO, YOU'LL NEVER FIND OUT WHY THE TOWER WON'T STAND.

DRAIN IT! THERE'S A BOX UNDER THERE!

HE NEVER WAS MUCH OF A WIZARD. . . . WHAT DOES THIS MEAN?

IT MEANS YOUR TOWER WILL STAND, BUT THAT YOU WON'T ENJOY ITS PROTECTION FOR LONG.

WHAT DO YOU MEAN?

THE RED DRAGON STANDS FOR KING UTHER PENDRAGON. HE WILL BE HERE SOON. HE HAS HEARD THAT YOU WANT HIS CROWN AND HIS KINGDOM, AND HE IS NOT HAPPY. THE WHITE DRAGON STOOD FOR YOU, VORTIGERN. SOON YOU'LL BE DEAD, LIKE IT. . . .

GUARDS!

HE HUNTS THE SOULS OF DEAD MEN WHO HAVE LIVED EVIL LIVES, AND CARRIES THEM OFF TO HIS LAIR BENEATH THE EARTH. . . .

WHY ARE YOU SHOWING ME THIS?

BECAUSE ARAWN DESIRES SOMETHING THAT YOU MAY ONE DAY CLAIM. IT IS BEST YOU KNOW OF HIM NOW. HE IS A TERRIBLE ADVERSARY. EVEN I CANNOT PROTECT YOU FROM HIM.

YOU'RE ALWAYS HINTING AT THINGS, MERLIN. WHEN WILL I GET TO LEARN WHAT THEY REALLY ARE?

SOON.

DUSK . . .

41

WHAT . . . !

GREETINGS, MIGHTY ONE!

WHAT WAS THAT?

AN OLD FRIEND. YOU'LL MEET HIM PROPERLY—SOON.

WHY NOT NOW? OH!

44

48

49

MERLIN! WHERE ARE YOU? MONSTERS! THEY'VE TAKEN MABON!

53

GLATISANT! GLATISANT! I NEED YOUR HELP!

MONSTERS HAVE TAKEN MABON.... I—I THINK THEY THOUGHT HE WAS ME. WHAT CAN I DO? MERLIN IS GONE!

ARTHUR, I CANNOT LEAVE THE WOOD. BUT THERE ARE OTHERS ... OLD FRIENDS ... THEY WILL HELP YOU....

WHERE CAN I FIND THEM? WHO ARE THEY?

THE PLACE WHERE YOU FIRST MET MABON. LOOK WITHIN THE POOL AND CALL TO THEM. SALMON, BLACKBIRD, EAGLE, AND STAG.

SALMON, GREAT ONE ... BLACKBIRD ... MIGHTY STAG ... EAGLE. PLEASE! I NEED YOUR HELP....

COLD . . .
SO . . .
COLD . . .

HOLD ON, ARTHUR. WE ARE ALMOST THERE.

WE MUST DEPART QUICKLY BEFORE MORE AND WORSE ENEMIES COME AFTER US.

THANK YOU, ARTHUR, AND YOU ALSO, OLD ONE, FOR COMING IN SEARCH OF ME. I SHALL BE WELL AGAIN SOON.

BLACKBIRD, YOU HAVE MY THANKS. I HEAR THE SONG OF THE GOLDEN WOOD. YOUR POWER'S ARE NOTHING, SERVANTS OF AMANGONS!

DO NOT HURT ME, MASTER!

I HEAR YOU HAVE A NEW MASTER NOW. . . .

AIEEEE!

MERLIN. . . .

HE CANNOT HELP YOU NOW.

IT IS NOTHING. CLIMB ON MY BACK.

EAGLE, YOU'RE HURT!

MERLIN . . . STAG . . .

WE SHALL JOIN YOU LATER. GET YOURSELVES AWAY. RETURN TO AVALON. TAKE THE WAY I SHOWED YOU.

BE CAREFUL!

THE LORD OF ANNWN IS TOO STRONG!

WHY WOULD HE DO THAT?

WE ARE OLD ENEMIES. AND I SENSE THAT HE SEEKS YOUR DEATH ALSO.

I FEAR THERE IS NOTHING WE CAN DO. THE WOUND IS TOO DEEP.

CAN WE HELP HIM?

I SHOULDN'T HAVE BROUGHT YOU HERE!

HE . . .
SHALL . . . NOT . . .
HAVE . . . US . . .
TODAY. . . .

TAKE CARE,
ARTHUR.
YOU WILL BE A
GREAT KING.

SOB!

I DON'T WANT TO BE KING. I'D RATHER STAY HERE WITH MY FRIENDS.

A TROUBLESOME WIZARD AND SOME ANIMALS . . . SCARCELY FIT COMPANY FOR A KING.

THE SWORD WILL CHOOSE.

YOU INSULT US!

BE CAREFUL YOU DO NOT GO TOO FAR!

THE TIME HAS COME TO FREE THE SWORD.

BY WHAT RIGHT DO YOU DARE TO ASK THIS THING!

I ASK AS A TRUE GUARDIAN OF THE LAND OF ALBION. THIS BOY IS DESTINED TO BE KING. THE SWORD OF FIRE AND ICE IS RIGHTLY HIS.

THEY ARE MY FRIENDS!

YOU WERE NOT INVITED, WIZARD!

THE SWORD IS A PRIZE TOO GREAT TO BE TAKEN LIGHTLY!

YOU HAVE MEDDLED ONCE TOO OFTEN, WIZARD!

YOUR WORDS ARE HIGH-SOUNDING, YET YOU OFFER NO PROOF OF THESE THINGS.

YOU HAVE SEEN WHAT I HAVE SEEN. ARTHUR'S LIFE AND THE FUTURE OF THIS LAND ARE LINKED BY BONDS OLDER THAN ANY OF US. HE HAS PROVED HIMSELF AGAINST AMANGONS.

SKREE! SKREE!

BOW BEFORE ME!

IT'S ME . . . ARTHUR . . .

BEND YOUR NECK!

I THOUGHT WE WERE FRIENDS. . . .

WHO DARES CHALLENGE THE GREEN KNIGHT?

HE HAS SUCCEEDED.

WE MUST GIVE HIM THE SWORD!

THE TIME OF ARTHUR IS ALMOST HERE. . . .

WELL DONE, MY BOY. THE TIME IS NEAR. . . .

YOU HAVE PASSED THE TEST, ARTHUR! YOU STOOD YOUR GROUND, EVEN WHEN YOU WERE AFRAID.

REJOICE WHILE YOU MAY. SOON I SHALL HAVE YOU. THEN THE SWORD SHALL BE MINE!

WHO
SAID THAT?

WE VOUCH FOR HIM!

HE WILL DRAW THE SWORD FROM THE STONE. HE WILL PROVE HIMSELF WORTHY.

BEHOLD THE KING!

THUS WAS BORN THE LEGEND OF KING ARTHUR. MANY ADVENTURES LAY BEFORE HIM. HE WOULD ESTABLISH THE GREAT ROUND TABLE AT CAMELOT AND CREATE A FELLOWSHIP OF HEROES, SUCH AS THE WORLD HAD NEVER SEEN.

WITH MERLIN AT HIS SIDE AND WITH THE PROTECTION OF THE NINE, HE WOULD COMBAT THE EVIL OF AMANGONS AND THE GREED OF ARAWN TO LEAVE BEHIND A STORY THAT ENDURES FOREVER.